LifeTimes

The Story of Pablo Picasso

by Liz Gogerly
illustrated by L. R. Galante

Thameside Press

Distributed in the United States by
Smart Apple Media
1980 Lookout Drive
North Mankato, MN 56003

Produced for Thameside Press by
White-Thomson Publishing Ltd
2/3 St Andrew's Place
Lewes, BN7 1UP, England.

© White-Thomson Publishing Limited 2002
Text copyright © Liz Gogerly 2002
Illustrations copyright © L. R. Galante 2002

ISBN 1-931983-17-8

Library of Congress Control Number 2002 141330

Editor: Kay Barnham
Designer: John Jamieson
Language consultant: Norah Granger, Senior Lecturer in
  Primary Education, University of Brighton, England.
Art consultant: Felicity Allen, Head of Public Programs,
  Hayward Gallery, London.

Printed in China

Introduction

Pablo Ruiz Picasso was born in Málaga, on the south coast of Spain, on October 25, 1881. His father, José Ruiz Blasco, was an art teacher, and it was from him that Pablo learned to draw. By the time Pablo was 15 it was clear that he was gifted. Later, while living in Barcelona among other artists and poets, his talent grew.

When Pablo was 19, one of his paintings was chosen for the 1900 World Exhibition in Paris. This was a great honor. With his friend, the artist Carlos Casagemas, Pablo traveled to the French capital city. Paris was the center of the art world, and the two young men were ready to be inspired. . . .

The City of Color

"What beautiful faces!" muttered Pablo, as he watched the young women in the dance hall. "Don't you think so?" he added to his friend Carlos.

"You love everything about this city," replied Carlos, with a shrug of his shoulders.

The pretty girls were just a part of the magic of Paris. At night, with the gaslights burning, this bustling city made you feel alive.

That night they were in Montmartre, which was like a small village on the outskirts of the city. Many artists had lived there, including Van Gogh and Toulouse-Lautrec. There were also cafés where people talked all night about art and poetry. Pablo loved it.

"I would like to paint this dance hall," Pablo exclaimed. "It's so full of life."

Carlos nodded, a small smile brightening his face for a moment.

"I can't go back to Spain when there's so much I could learn here," continued Pablo, his eyes gleaming. "I think Paris is where I will become a great artist, Carlos."

"And," added Carlos, "a great talker!"

That fall, Pablo and Carlos
were living in a top-floor studio in
Montmartre. They'd moved there to
be close to their Spanish artist friends
who lived in that part of the city.

But Pablo loved all of Paris. When
he saw the Eiffel Tower and the
wonderful displays at the World
Exhibition, Pablo felt a buzz of
excitement flow through him.
Everywhere he went, he had
the same feeling.

Some days he visited exhibitions by famous
Impressionist and Post-impressionist painters.
He spent hours admiring the works of Degas,
Gauguin, Van Gogh, and Toulouse-Lautrec.

On other days he would wander around the
Louvre, France's greatest art gallery. Many
people came to see the famous paintings, but
Pablo was more interested in the ancient art of
the Egyptians and the Greeks. Everything he
did, and everywhere he went, Pablo felt as if
his imagination was on fire.

It was a sunny day in Montmartre, and the light flooded from the window onto Pablo's latest painting.

"I like it," said Carlos. "It has a touch of Toulouse-Lautrec about it, and er. . ." —Carlos felt Pablo's eyes boring into him— "and Pablo Picasso, of course!"

Pablo was suddenly thoughtful. "True," he said. "It does remind me of Toulouse-Lautrec."

"There's nothing wrong with taking ideas from great painters, Pablo," replied Carlos.

"I know, but. . ." Pablo didn't look satisfied.

"And, Pedro Mañach wants to give you 150 francs for all your work—you're doing really well!"

"He's just buying them because he's my friend!" Pablo exclaimed. Then he looked serious. "I just want to find my own style."

"You will. . . ." said Carlos.

The catch in his voice made Pablo look closer at his friend. "Are you OK, Carlos?"

"Yes," Carlos answered, too quickly. Both knew this wasn't true. Carlos was in love with a girl who didn't love him. He was heartbroken.

"Everything will be all right," Pablo reassured Carlos. "She'll change her mind."

From the 1860s onward, Impressionist painters like Monet, Renoir, and Degas had influenced artists around the world. They painted everyday scenes of country and city life, but they used bright colors and tried new ways of brushing paint onto the canvas. Some people thought the paintings looked unfinished, while others liked their simplicity and use of light. Post-impressionist artists like Paul Gauguin and Van Gogh used bolder colors and discovered new techniques. Picasso borrowed ideas from many of these artists.

A World in Blue

It was summer 1901. The Parisian cafés were as lively as ever. The familiar sound of the accordion and the constant chatter spilled out onto the cobbled streets. Sunshine brought warmth and light to every crowded corner. Pablo and his friend Mañach were sitting in a small café.

"So Ambroise Vollard likes your work?" said Mañach, beaming. "He's one of the best dealers in Paris."

"It's great news," Pablo agreed, but without excitement.

"He's sponsored really famous artists and now he wants to exhibit *your* work!"

Pablo still looked blank.

"I know. It's just that I can't stop thinking about Carlos's suicide. It's like a little light has been switched off deep down inside me. Sometimes, when I think about him, my mood is so black," Pablo said quietly. "Other times, when I'm painting well I can forget the pain."

"You must think of yourself and your talent now," Mañach said. "Carlos would want you to be successful."

Pablo's exhibition was a success.

"The critics are saying you'll be the next Toulouse-Lautrec or Degas," Mañach exclaimed, his face lighting up with pride.

"I don't want to be the next anyone else," grinned Pablo. "I want to be Pablo Picasso!"

"Let's drink to that, then," said Mañach as he raised his glass.

As the summer wore on, Pablo's confidence grew. He visited cabarets and clubs with his Spanish artist friends. He'd also made new friends, like the French poet, Max Jacob.

Life was busy, but Pablo always found time to watch the world go by. In his head, he collected images of poor women in shabby clothes or children begging.

Back in the studio, the images were quickly brought back to life using colors that expressed both his wonder and sadness for ordinary people—shades of blue and green. Soon, these colors took over his paintings.

"Why do you use so much blue?" asked Max Jacob one day.

"It adds emotion, don't you think?" Pablo replied.

"Yes," Max agreed. "Everyone looks more lonely and lost."

"I only wish Vollard and Mañach liked them," Pablo mumbled. "They haven't bought anything for months. I can hardly afford to eat."

"I'll buy lunch," Max offered.

Pablo patted Max's shoulder. "Thanks," he said, "but I think I know somebody who will buy my paintings. . . ."

Later that day, Pablo set off with a canvas under his arm. He headed for the junk shop up the street.

"This is good!" The shopkeeper studied the painting. It was of a neat attic room bathed in blue shadows. The bed, with sheets peeled back, was blue. The bathtub where the ghostly-looking girl was washing was blue. It was a sad picture, but the shopkeeper liked it.

"I wish I could afford more than 20 francs," he said.

"That's what I need just to eat'" replied Pablo angrily. He hated parting with his pictures for so little money.

Pablo returned to Barcelona, but no one wanted his blue pictures there, either. By the summer of 1902, he was eager to be back in Paris. But he felt very low. Would he ever settle down or make any money?

By now, he couldn't even afford to rent a room.

Luckily, his friend Max took pity on him and invited him to stay.

"It's your turn to sleep," laughed Max as he leaped out of bed. He rubbed his eyes in disbelief. "Have you really been painting all night, Pablo?"

"Well, it's better than worrying about my rumbling stomach," Pablo said, yawning deeply, "or my tired eyes."

"I'm not surprised your eyes hurt when you have only one candle to paint by," Max said. He looked concerned.

"Don't worry, Max." Pablo slumped onto the bed. "I'm going to be famous one day, and I'll have electric lights to paint by."

". . . And we'll eat in the best restaurants," Max added.

". . . And all my dreams will come true." Pablo closed his eyes. Before long, he was fast asleep.

Picasso's Blue Period lasted from 1901 until 1905. During these years Picasso traveled between Paris and Barcelona looking for a place to settle down. His paintings showed many of the poor people from the two cities. Paintings such as *Child Holding a Dove*, *The Tragedy*, *The Blue Room* (described on page 15), and *The Old Guitarist* have a sadness that is felt in all of his work from this time. Another important Blue Period painting was *The Burial of Casagemas*, in which Picasso paid tribute to his friend Carlos.

Like a Rose

"Come on, babies," Pablo called to his scruffy dogs, Gat, Feo, and Frika. "I'll find you some food." With that, he began sorting through a trash can for scraps.

"I know," he cooed. "I'm hungry, too."

In the past months, Pablo had begun to feel happier with his life in Montmartre, even though he struggled to feed himself. Now he looked up the hill to the ugly building that his friends had nicknamed the *Bateau Lavoir*. True, it looked like one of the laundry barges on the River Seine, but it was his home. Once it had been a piano factory, but now it housed artists and writers.

There was no electricity or gas. There was
one grubby toilet and one leaky faucet. But
Pablo loved the old place.

There were other reasons to be happy, too.
Pablo had his own studio again. It smelled of
turpentine and paint, but it was the meeting
place for his friends. Max dropped by often, as
did the poets Guillaume Apollinaire and André
Salmon. And, of course, there was Fernande—
his new girlfriend. Hopefully they'd all be
waiting for him at the *Bateau Lavoir* now.

"I know!" There was a mischievous glint in Pablo's eyes as he looked at the friends lounging around his studio. "Let's go to *Le Lapin Agile.*"

"We won't get get away without paying again," Guillaume said, looking doubtful.

Pablo dusted off his worn-out jacket and ran paint-covered fingers through the dark hair that now reached his collar.

"How could they refuse such fine customers?" Pablo exclaimed.

Everyone laughed. It was the same every
evening—a guessing game as to who would
be stupid enough to let them pay another day.
Usually Pablo's charm ensured that he and his
friends had something to eat.

Later, as they sat outside the café, Pablo
breathed in the warm night air. He felt utterly
happy. A tasty dinner had been followed by a
poetry reading. Then the owner's daughter had
brought out her tame crow to hop among the
customers, making one woman scream. Pablo
and his friends had laughed until they cried.
Life in Montmartre was never dull.

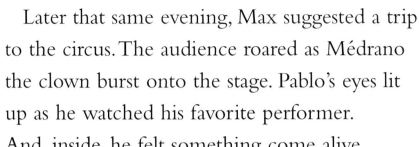

Later that same evening, Max suggested a trip
to the circus. The audience roared as Médrano
the clown burst onto the stage. Pablo's eyes lit
up as he watched his favorite performer.
And, inside, he felt something come alive.

In the following weeks Pablo made friends
with the acrobats, harlequins, strongmen,
and bareback riders. He was
inspired by their colorful
lives, and before long he
started to paint them.

"The colors are magnificent," said Guillaume, looking at the large canvas propped up against the wall. Pablo had painted a family of acrobats. There was an air of mystery about the family, who did not speak or look at each other. . . .

"You've made everyone look alone," Guillaume said, looking at the picture thoughtfully, "and yet it isn't a sad picture."

"The rose colors give it light, don't you think?" suggested Pablo.

"I'm sure that you'll sell these paintings," agreed Guillaume.

As the pinks and grays took over from
the blues in his paintings, Pablo's fame grew.
He didn't want to exhibit his work, but he was
happy to sell to collectors like the American
art lovers Leo and Gertrude Stein. Hearing
of his genius, they braved the dirty corridors
of the *Bateau Lavoir*. They soon became regular
visitors to Pablo's studio.

"Thank you for your support, dear Guillaume,"
exclaimed Pablo. He was opening a bottle of
wine—today was going to be a celebration.

"Even I didn't expect Vollard to buy 20 paintings!" said Guillaume delightedly.

"And can you believe the Steins spent 800 francs!" Pablo was shaking with excitement. "I'll never have to ask for a free meal again."

"Here's to your future," said Guillaume, raising his glass.

"Cheers!" Pablo lifted his glass, too. "Here's to success."

In 1904, Picasso finally made Paris his home, and the next year his Rose Period began. He now used warmer colors such as pinks and shades of red. *The Family of Saltimbanques* (pages 22–23) is a famous painting from this time. In 1905, Leo Stein bought his first painting by Picasso. With his sister Gertrude he started an art collection that also included the works of Matisse, the French painter. By May 1906, Ambroise Vollard was buying Picasso's paintings and selling them to collectors. Picasso's days as a poor, hungry artist were over.

Painting Gertrude

"You can't paint her face like that," Max said, looking shocked.

Pablo was silent. He'd wanted to give Gertrude a portrait of herself in return for her support, but it was proving to be difficult. He'd now been painting Gertrude Stein for months—she'd sat patiently for more than 80 sessions—yet all he'd managed to paint was her large, rounded figure. . . . What about her face?

No matter how he tried, he couldn't capture Gertrude's serious expression. Again and again he wiped away his efforts, until one day he'd had enough.

"I can't see you any longer when I look,"
he snapped.

Pablo returned to Spain for a few months,
while the unfinished portrait gathered dust.

In a flash, Pablo had now felt inspired to
pick up his brushes and finish her face.
Even if Max disapproved, he was pleased
with the result.

"Her face looks like a mask!" exclaimed Max.

"It looks like one of those ancient sculptures," said Guillaume.

"She looks so hard," Fernande couldn't help adding. "I don't think she'll like that!"

"She'll understand," Pablo said confidently. He was pleased with the result. It was simple, yet somehow it said so much more about Gertrude than a true likeness ever would. Gertrude was due any moment, and he was looking forward to giving her the portrait.

Minutes later, Gertrude was silent as she gazed at the image of herself.

Then she turned to Pablo and smiled. "You've done it again. This is marvelous."

Everyone, including Pablo, sighed with relief.

"Why, I will put this up in my living room for all to see," Gertrude continued. "People will come and they will ask who did this. I'll smile with pride and tell them that it was painted by the genius of all geniuses—Pablo Picasso!"

Picasso painted Gertrude Stein in the spring of 1906. The masklike image was shocking to many people, but for Picasso it was an important change of style. He told his friends, "everybody thinks she is not at all like her portrait but never mind, in the end she will manage to look just like it." Gertrude kept the painting for the rest of her life. Some people agreed that as the years went by Gertrude did look more like the portrait, so Picasso's imagination was proved to be more powerful than a painting of a true likeness.

Breaking All the Rules

One sunny day, André and Guillaume were walking up the hill toward Pablo's studio. They were trying to figure out what had been keeping Picasso so busy.

"He's been sketching and painting like mad for months," Guillaume said. "Has he shown you what's he's up to?"

André shook his head. "No—it's a mystery to me"

As the two men approached the square below the *Bateau Lavoir*, they saw Pablo crouching on the ground.

He was surrounded by a group of ragged
children. All eyes were fixed on the outlines of
animals that Pablo had been tracing in the dust.

"One more," begged a little girl. "Please
draw a rabbit."

André and Guillaume joined the huddled
group, fascinated by their friend's talent.

"Good day!" Pablo rose to greet his friends.
"Max and Fernande are waiting upstairs.
Come and see what I've been painting."

There was feeling of excitement in the studio. In the corner, a large canvas was turned away from everybody. They couldn't wait to see Pablo's latest masterpiece.

"So," said Max, "let us in on the secret."

Pablo's face was flushed with excitement as he gently edged the huge canvas around. His friends stared with unbelieving eyes. They shuffled uncomfortably as they took in the five women in the painting who seemed to glare back at them.

"Well. . . ." André was
the only one brave enough to speak.
"They're quite frightening. . . ."

These women were not beautiful; they
didn't even look like real women. Their bodies
seemed to be made of geometric shapes.
Two faces looked like African masks, while
the others were lopsided. One woman in the
corner had her back to them, yet her head
faced forward. No one had ever seen anything
like it before.

A silence fell on the group. More than one
of them wondered why Pablo had painted such
a strange picture. Why would somebody who
painted so beautifully suddenly produce
something so crude? Why would he change
his style so much, just as he was becoming
successful?

Pablo could tell that his friends were puzzled.

"I wanted to paint something that showed
what I think about an object, as well as how
I see it," he tried to explain.

"Oh, Pablo," Guillaume muttered quietly.
"Do you think people will understand?"

"I don't paint for other people!" Pablo barked.

"I've been looking for my own style for so long now. Here, at last, is something I can call my own. It might be shocking, but it says so much more than anything I've ever done before!"

"You'll certainly cause a stir this time," Max sighed.

"Mmmm," said Fernande, shuffling closer to Pablo. "I'm sure people will understand. I think it's marvelous."

Some people believe that this painting is the beginning of modern art. It was named *Les Demoiselles d'Avignon* ("The Young Women of Avignon") by Picasso's friend André Salmon. When it was finished, in 1907, some of the people whom Picasso invited to view the painting spoke out against it, including his rival, the artist Henri Matisse. They disliked the harsh, jagged edges of his subjects, and the fact that this was different from anything ever painted before. Picasso didn't exhibit the painting until 1916, when its importance was finally recognized.

The Shattered Mirror

After five years at the *Bateau Lavoir,* Pablo
moved on. He was now rich enough to rent a
large apartment on the boulevard de Clichy—
a more fashionable part of Paris. He could
have moved sooner, but the thought of leaving
Montmartre and his friends had held him back.

"It's so light and spacious, Pablo," Fernande
laughed as she ran from the studio to the
bedroom. "And finally we have a separate room
to sleep in, and room for a maid."

36

"There's space for the animals too," Pablo added. Besides his collection of junk, he'd insisted they bring all their pets—a mob that now included a few cats, a monkey called Mamina, and yet more dogs.

"Now," said Pablo as he began sorting through his collection of strangely shaped bottles, old musical instruments, and pieces of African art, "we must find a home for all this—then I can begin to paint again!"

Pablo's friends often walked from Montmartre down the hill to his new apartment. One of the most regular visitors was the artist Georges Braque. Very soon the two men became close friends.

Locking themselves away in their studios they would spend hours exchanging ideas.

One day, Pablo looked thoughtfully at Georges's latest painting. It was made up of lots of cubes and geometric shapes. "You know," he said, "it's getting difficult to tell our work apart."

"Mmm," Georges agreed. "I don't know who started to paint like this first."

"It doesn't really matter," Pablo said. "We've both discovered something important."

"Yes," laughed his friend. "We're like two rock climbers roped together."

"...On the way to the top'" Pablo added with a glint in his eyes, "with our own new style."

He wasn't being bigheaded. Artists from all around the world had started to copy their work. The two painters had invented a style that was being called "cubism."

One day, the art dealer Daniel-Henry
Kahnweiler came to visit Pablo's studio.
It wasn't his first visit. Pablo had been painting
him for some weeks; earlier that day he'd
added the final touches.

"I'm looking forward to this," Kahnweiler
said slightly nervously.

"I hope it's one you'll be happy to add to
your collection," said Pablo. He turned the
portrait around for Kahnweiler to see.

Kahnweiler knew enough about Pablo's style
to expect something different, and he wasn't
shocked by the geometric shapes that formed
him. But he was stunned by the brilliance
of this new style.

Pablo had painted Kahnweiler's portrait as if he were seeing him from every angle. His eyes, his smiling mouth, even his hands, all appeared in fragments. The effect was something like looking through a shattered mirror.

"This," said Kahnweiler excitedly, "is a perfect example of cubism!"

Later, Pablo thought about his friend's reaction. What would he think of his next idea?

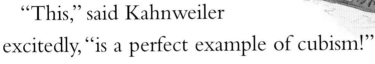

In *Les Demoiselles d'Avignon*, Picasso painted his subject as if he were looking at it from different sides. That's why the women looked as if they'd been broken into weird shapes and angles. From 1908 on, he worked with Georges Braque and developed this style using dull colors such as muddy browns, greens, and grays. Sometimes it was hard to tell what the painting was supposed to be. Soon, people began to call their style "cubism" because the subjects appeared to be broken down into little cubes.

What Next?

As time went on, Pablo and Braque played with more new ideas.

"You're so bold," enthused Kahnweiler as he looked at Pablo's latest picture. Pablo had glued pieces of music and newspaper, and a drawing of a glass together. It wasn't a drawing of a guitar, but a picture that looked like a guitar. "Yet again, you've done something nobody else would dare," Picasso's friend sighed.

"It's just collage," said Pablo modestly, "but it makes you think, doesn't it?"

Kahnweiler was thinking. Most artists would be content to have discovered a new style and then stuck to it. Not so with Pablo Picasso. His brilliant imagination had brought him fame and fortune. Yet, instead of touring the world, meeting famous people, here he was, waiting for his old friends.

Soon, Pablo's friends arrived at the café. It was just like old times. Everyone wanted to eat, drink, and see what fun Montmartre had to offer tonight.

"Pierre!" Pablo called to the musician in the corner of the café. "May I borrow your guitar?"

"You can't play that thing," Max said.

"Oh, can't I?" Pablo answered. He had a mischievous glint in his eye. Slowly, he turned the guitar upside down and ran his small hand along the curve of the instrument.

"If you look at it like this," he said, raising his eyebrows, "it looks like a woman's body." All his friends began giggling like schoolboys. "But," he continued, "look closer. . . ."

Everyone leaned in to look at the guitar. "Now, it could be a face."

"Oh, yes," laughed Andre. "The hole looks like a mouth. . . and the strings are a bit like a nose."

"You see!" Pablo looked thrilled. "You can see it too. And that has inspired me!"

"What will you think of next?" asked Guillaume, looking puzzled.

"Well," Pablo's eyes lit up with a familiar glow as his friends waited to hear of his latest idea. "You'll just have to wait and see. . . ."

By 1912, Picasso and Braque were developing new ways of painting everyday objects. Pictures such as *Violin* and *Grapes* were brighter, and it was easier to recognize the subject of the painting. Collage was a development from this style. In his picture *Guitar, Sheet Music, and Wine Glass*, Picasso used pieces of sheet music, newspaper, and a sketch of a wine glass. Later, he experimented with sculpture. Yet again Picasso had found a new and clever way of showing everyday things.

Picasso's Life and Art

Picasso left Paris in the 1940s, to move to the south of France. Throughout his long and colorful life he never lost his passion for art, his love of women and children, and his loyalty to good friends and animals. Picasso became the most famous and popular artist of the twentieth century. By the age of 65 he was a millionaire.

During the rest of his life, Pablo Picasso changed his style and invented new forms of art. Though he explored modern and classical styles, and often stole ideas from painters and sculptors, his work always inspired other artists.

Besides painting and sculpture, he designed costumes and sets for the ballet; he made pottery and prints; he even wrote poetry and a play. One of his most famous paintings is *Guernica*, which shows his horror at the bombing of a village during the Spanish Civil War. Many consider this to be the greatest work of his long career.

Timeline

1881	October 25. Pablo Ruiz Picasso is born in Malaga, Spain.
1895	Picasso's family moves to Barcelona; Picasso goes to art school.
1900	Visits Paris for the first time.
1901	Blue Period begins.
1904	Settles in Paris.
1905	Blue Period ends, and he paints *Family of Saltimbanques*.
1906	Rose Period begins, and he paints *Portrait of Gertrude Stein*.
1907	Rose Period ends, and he paints *Les Desmoiselles d'Avignon*.
1908	Develops cubist art with Georges Braque.
1910	Paints *Portrait of Kahnweiler*.
1914–18	First World War.
1917	Designs the set for Diaghilev's ballet *Parade*.
1918	Marries Russian ballet dancer Olga Koklova.
1919	Paints classical nudes.
1925	Picasso's style becomes more distorted and violent, yet more inventive.
1936	Spanish Civil War begins.
1937	Paints *Guernica*.
1939–45	Second World War.
1946	Picasso moves to the south of France.
1947	Begins work on ceramics.
1961	Picasso marries Jacqueline Roque and lives a less public life.
1973	April 8. Dies in France.

More Information

Books to read
Art for Young People: Pablo Picasso by
Matthew Meadows (Sterling, 1996)
Introducing Picasso by Juliet Heslewood
(Little Brown, 1993)
The Life and Works of Picasso by
Nathaniel Harris (Shooting Star Press,
1994)

Websites
http://www.tamu.edu/mocl/picasso
http://www.showgate.com/tots/
picasso/piclink.html

Museums
In his long career Picasso created
thousands of works of art. Museums
all around the world have examples of
his work. Here are just a few:

Picasso Museum, Barcelona, Spain.
The Picasso Museum, Paris, France.
The Tate Modern, London, England.
Museum of Modern Art, New York,
N.Y.
National Gallery of Art, Washington,
D.C.

Glossary

canvas Strong, coarse cloth, usually
stretched over a wooden frame to
create a surface on which to paint.
caricature A picture of somebody
that exaggerates their features so they
look comical or ugly.
classical A traditional or accepted
style.
collage A picture made by sticking
paper, cloth, or any other material
onto a surface.

geometric Describes a regular shape
such as a circle, triangle, square, or
rectangle.
harlequin A clown who wears a
mask and a multicolored costume.
Impressionist An artistic style that
aims to give an impression of a scene,
by use of color and light.
primitive An early or ancient
civilization. Also used to describe a
simple style of art.

Index

Bateau Lavoir	18, 19, 24, 30, 36	Louvre	7
Braque, Georges	38, 41, 42, 45, 47		
		portraits	26, 27, 28, 29, 40, 41, 47
circus	22		
collage	43, 45, 48	Montmartre	5, 6, 8, 18, 21, 36, 38, 44
cubism	39, 41		
Eiffel Tower	6	sculpture	28, 45, 46
Impressionists	7, 9, 48	World Exhibition	3, 6

48